SNOW LION

by David McPhail

PARENTS MAGAZINE PRESS
NEW YORK

For Caitlin

Library of Congress Cataloging in Publication Data
McPhail, David M.   Snow lion.
Summary: Lion, finding the jungle too hot for comfort, visits the mountains and falls in love with the cold fluffy white snow that covers the ground there.
[1. Lions — Fiction. 2. Jungle animals — Fiction.
3. Snow — Fiction] I. Title.
PZ7.M2427Sn   1983   [E]   82-8119
ISBN 0-8193-1097-2   AACR2
ISBN 0-8193-1098-0   (lib. bdg.)

A Parents Magazine
READ ALOUD Original.

Lion lived in the jungle.
It was hot in the jungle,
too hot for Lion.

It was too hot to chase zebras.
It was too hot to tumble in the grass.

It was too hot to do anything
but lie in the shade and pant.
Lion was doing just that when
his friend, Elephant, stopped by.
"It's hot," said Elephant.

Lion was too hot to talk.
He just nodded his head
ever-so-slightly.

Elephant could see that Lion wanted to be left alone, so he went away.

Soon after, Mrs. Baboon came along
with her children.
They climbed all over Lion.

They tugged his mane
and pulled his whiskers.
"Aren't they darling?" said Mrs. Baboon.
"They just love to play!"

But Lion was in no mood to play.
He just growled —
a low, rumbling growl
that startled Mrs. Baboon.

"Come along, children," she called.
"I don't think Mr. Lion
wants to play today."

Lion closed his eyes and tried to sleep.
But it was even too hot for that.

Suddenly, Lion jumped up.

"I know," he said. "I'll go away.
It must be cool *somewhere*."

So he packed his toothbrush and comb,
and slowly left the jungle.

Lion walked and walked.

When the sun went down,
the jungle was far behind him.

It was dark and cool in the hills.

Lion wasn't hot anymore,
but he was very tired.
He lay down and fell fast asleep.

When Lion woke up,
he was shivering with cold.
All around him was a soft,
white blanket.

Lion could only see
the tip of his tail.

Lion stood and shook himself.
He scooped up a pawful
of the soft white stuff.

He smelled it. It had no smell.
He tasted it. It had no taste.

Lion walked a few steps.
His footsteps followed him.

Then he began to run ...

He tried to stop,
but he slipped and went flying!

Lion landed with a PLOMPF!
"What fun!" he shouted. "Yippee!"

Then Lion had an idea.
He would take some of the lovely
cool softness back home
to share with his friends.
"They will love it!" roared Lion.
So he filled his suitcase with fluff
and headed down to the jungle.

As soon as he got back,
Lion saw Elephant and Mrs. Baboon.
"Look what I have!" he called to them.

"What is it?" they asked.
"You'll see,"
Lion said proudly.

A crowd of animals gathered 'round.
Lion opened his suitcase
and turned it upside down.
But all that fell out were a comb,
a toothbrush, and some water
that made a little puddle
on the hot
jungle
ground.

Lion looked into the suitcase.
"It was filled with cold fluffy stuff,"
he said.
"I found it in the hills."

"Of course you did," said the animals.
And, shaking their heads,
they walked away.

Lion was puzzled.
What had happened to his treasure?
He wished he had some now
to put on his head,
for he felt hotter than ever.
Lion spent the rest of the day
thinking about the fluffy stuff.

Finally, he decided to go
back to the hills for some more.
This time, he would put
a lock on his suitcase
so the fluffy stuff couldn't get out!

It took Lion all day and night
to go to the hills and come back.

When he returned, Lion called
to the animals again.

"Gather 'round, friends!" he shouted.
"This time you *will* see the cold,
white, fluffy stuff!"

He unlocked the suitcase
and turned it upside down.
Only water splashed out.
The animals shook their heads sadly.
"Poor Lion," they said.
"The heat finally got to him."

Lion was very unhappy.
He went away to hide and think.
Suddenly the answer came to him.

"The cold white fluffy stuff can't
come to the jungle — it's too hot here!
The fluffy stuff can live
only where it's cold!
Follow me!" he called to the animals.

At first the animals would not go.
Then Elephant said, "We must follow Lion
because he is our friend.
And besides, a walk will be fun."

So off they went,
with Lion leading the way.

As soon as they reached the hills,
they began to feel cooler.

Lion ran ahead.
He made balls of the fluffy stuff
and threw them at his friends.

The animals threw some back at Lion.
They slipped and slid
and fell and laughed.

They pushed giant balls
of fluff down the hill.

Then, while Elephant played with Lion,
the rest of the animals went to work.
They made something very big ...

"This is for you, Lion!" they said.
"It is to thank you for bringing us
to this wonderful
place!"

The animals played some more.

Then finally, happy and tired,
they went home to the jungle.

But on the hottest days,
they always go back.